# Cosmo
## THE DODO BIRD™

# COSMO
## THE DODO BIRD™

Cosmo is a dodo bird, a unique species that lived on Earth 300 years ago. Cosmo lived with his family and beloved friends on the island of Mauritius, a paradise isolated from the world known to man.

When the first humans arrived on the island, the dodos' environment changed vastly, and it wasn't long before almost all of the dodos completely disappeared.

Now, Cosmo is the last of his kind on Earth.

3R-V is a small robot-spaceship from the future, built to save extinct species. During his very first mission, he accidentally landed on Mauritius and met Cosmo, the last of the dodos. They decided that they would travel the universe looking for dodos. They found many adventures along the way, but did they discover any dodos? Read and find out!

Originally published as *Les Aventures de Cosmo le dodo de l'espace: La quête du dernier dodo* by Origo Publications, POB 4, Chambly, Quebec J3L 4B1, 2008

Library of Congress Control Number: 2010928803

**Library and Archives Canada Cataloguing in Publication**
Pat Rac, 1963-
[Quête du dernier dodo. English]
The quest of the last dodo bird / Patrice Racine.

(The adventures of Cosmo – the dodo bird)
Translation of: La quête du dernier dodo.
For ages 8-11.

ISBN 978-1-77049-241-7

I. Title.  II. Title: Quête du dernier dodo.  English.
III. Series: Pat Rac, 1963- .  Adventures of cosmo the dodo bird – our hero of the environment.

PS8631.A8294Q4813 2011        jC843'.6        C2010-903180-6

We acknowledge the financial support of the Government of Canada through the Book Publishing Industry Development Program (BPIDP) and that of the Government of Ontario through the Ontario Media Development Corporation's Ontario Book Initiative. We further acknowledge the support of the Canada Council for the Arts and the Ontario Arts Council for our publishing program.

**ONTARIO ARTS COUNCIL**
**CONSEIL DES ARTS DE L'ONTARIO**

*For information on international rights, please visit www.cosmothedododbird.com.*

Printed in Mexico

1 2 3 4 5 6        16 15 14 13 12 11

MIX
Paper from
responsible sources
FSC
www.fsc.org  FSC® C101537

For all the children of the world

# THE QUEST

## OF THE LAST DODO BIRD

N

W E

S

*Mauritius Island*

TUNDRA BOOKS

# Table of Contents

# Mauritius

I hid behind a tree to catch my breath. Zoe and Raoul were getting closer. I could hear the sound of their steps.

I had no time to lose. I headed back into the forest, dodging branches, roots, and rocks, but suddenly I came to a ravine. How would I get across? I looked around and saw a fallen tree spanning the void. A bridge!

"I see him, Raoul!" Zoe called out, not far behind me.

I raced across the bridge. When I got to the other side, I pushed the tree trunk with all my might. It plunged into the ravine.

"Aha! That should stop you!" I crowed.

But Raoul was climbing another tree. Before I knew it, he had loosened a vine. Zoe grabbed it and swung across the ravine. I turned and ran. Then, I came to a wide, blue river. There was a rock path across it, and I hopped onto the closest boulder. I had to tread carefully. The setting sun was blinding me, and the rocks were slippery.

Halfway across, I heard a sound. It was Raoul, standing on a rock behind me. Somehow Zoe was already ahead of me. I was caught between them. There was only one thing to do.

I jumped into the water and swam toward the riverbank. Raoul did a cannonball into the water right after me.

Then Zoe dove in gracefully. I got to the bank first, but in no time, my way was blocked by a rocky cliff. I climbed as fast as I could, but I lost my footing and rolled all the way down to where Raoul and Zoe were waiting for me.

"Gotcha, Cosmo!" said Zoe.

"This time we nabbed you in no time at all!" Raoul boasted.

"Look back there!" I cried as I pointed to the river. "It's a monster!"

Zoe and Raoul peered behind them. Before they could turn back, I was up the rocks and circling back to our village.

If I could just touch my nest before Raoul and Zoe caught me, I'd win the race. "Excuse me! Sorry. Oops. Pardon!" I pushed my way past the other dodos, who were getting ready for the fast approaching night.

"There he is!" yelled Raoul.

I looked over my shoulder. "You won't catch me!"

And that's when I crashed into something. Or should I say, somebody.

"There you are, my little fluffball," Mom scolded me. "It's late. Where were you?"

"We were playing in the forest," I said.

Raoul and Zoe had caught up. They both nodded.

"Did you at least win the race, little one?"

"Yes."

"No, you didn't, Cosmo. You didn't touch your nest." Zoe was giggling.

My mother tapped my tail feathers. "Be quick now."

I slipped through her legs and ran. Zoe and Raoul followed me as I jumped into my nest. "I win!"

They leaped in after me. We had a tickle fight that made us laugh so hard we could barely catch our breath.

Then, it was time for Raoul and Zoe to go to their own nest. The last things I heard before I drifted off to sleep were Raoul's snores and Zoe's even breathing.

In the middle of the night, a solemn voice woke me.
I saw all the adults in the village gathered around the fire.
A stranger was among them.

I tiptoed close to the fire and saw an old dodo with
a crown of feathers on his head. One of his eyes was
missing, and in its place was a nasty scar. I shivered from
head to tail, but moved closer to listen.

"Creatures, walking on two feet, have landed on our
island. They are headed this way," said the stranger.

"Visitors! We have to get ready to welcome them,"
exclaimed Zoe's mother happily.

"You don't understand," cried the old dodo. "They are dangerous! They ruin everything in their paths. They have already destroyed the villages that were near the beach, including mine. And they brought rats with them to devour our eggs."

"What happened to the dodos?" my father asked.

"Gone. All of them, gone. I am the only survivor."

All the adults fell silent.

I was frightened.

"Cosmo?" My mother had noticed me. "What are you doing here?" I stepped out of the shadows and crawled into her arms.

"What kind of creatures are they?" I asked.

"Humans," the stranger said.

"Are they close?"

"Very close, little one. They'll be here by tomorrow at the latest."

CHAPTER ONE

# Hunted

"Did you hear that?" asked Zoe.

"Yes, we heard it." Raoul, Zoe, and I had taken refuge under a giant leaf to rest. All night long, hunters carrying nets had tracked us through the forest.

"Do you think the humans have found us?" Raoul sounded worried.

"Maybe it's just rats," said Zoe. "I double-dare them to come anywhere near me! I'll show them!" Zoe was ready for a fight, but Raoul held his sister back.

"What if it's another dodo?" I said.

"I wish it was. It's been ages since we've seen one," said Zoe sadly.

Another twig snapped, but this time it sounded closer. All of a sudden, I heard a call.

"It *is* another dodo!" I said.

"How can we be sure?" asked Zoe.

"Of course, it's another dodo!" Raoul cried.

We crept out from under the leaf. We looked around, but there was no sign of a dodo. Just then, a net dropped over my head. Another net captured Raoul and Zoe. We all struggled, but the nets held us tightly.

Two humans jumped out of the bushes. "So, we've got our dodos at last." The hunter who spoke was big and brawny.

The other was smaller, but more terrifying. "Your dodo call is getting better and better. I don't know what you're saying to them, but it sure gets them out of hiding."

"Thanks. Now let's take these game birds back to the boat."

They headed off, the brawny one carrying the net that held Zoe and Raoul captive and the little one carrying me with the net slung over his shoulder.

After some time, we came to the ocean where a massive ship was anchored close to shore. Sailors were busy on the bridge. Others sat in a boat filled with barrels of provisions for the ship's next voyage.

The men shoved us into a cage. "Here, take the key! Give it to Captain Tork," said the big one.

Captain Tork! That name terrified me. The last dodos we'd seen had told us about the heartless human. Zoe gripped my arm, and Raoul huddled closer.

We watched the two hunters make their way to the ship. A young man hurried toward them. He looked excitedly in our direction. "You captured the dodos? They are the only . . ."

"Of course, we did! Now get out of our way." The hunters pushed past the young man, knocking him down.

# CHAPTER TWO

# Marco the Brave

The hunters climbed into a boat and rowed toward the ship. The young man got up and brushed the sand from his red coat and blue pants. He groped for his glasses before speaking to us.

"Hello, I'm Marco," he said.

I gave him a wary look. Marco shook his head. "What on Earth am I doing? I'm talking to birds. . . ."

Perched on a stool, he grabbed a pad of paper and some charcoal. For a few seconds, he studied us. Then he started to draw.

At first, he worked in silence. When he spoke, his voice was kind. "I know that the sailors who have come to this island have been terribly cruel to you. They have almost destroyed your species. You're the last dodos on Mauritius – maybe even in the world!"

Zoe, Raoul, and I clutched each other. We couldn't believe it.

As he drew, Marco spoke to us. "What can I do to save you dodos? Maybe I could take you three to the king's palace. He has a big garden there, with lots of birds."

"What's a garden?" I whispered. Zoe and Raoul shrugged. They had no idea, either.

Marco continued. "The problem is that the climate there isn't adapted to your needs. Wait! What if I built a big cage and recreated your environment? *Hmmm*, I'll need samples of the plants that grow here."

Zoe, Raoul, and I were horrified. None of us wanted to live in a cage.

Marco continued mumbling to himself. I looked at his sketch pad, and I could see his drawing of a dodo. It looked just like us.

He was interrupted by a sneer. "What are you doing there, boy?"

CHAPTER THREE

# Perfect for a Feast

Captain Tork stood in front of us, flanked by our captors. "What are you up to?" He sounded impatient.

"Captain, Sir, I'm documenting my research," said Marco.

"By drawing them?"

"Did you know that thousands of dodos used to live on this island? These three are now the last of them."

"So?"

"It's unlikely that this unique species can be found anywhere else in the world."

"Unique? They're uniquely perfect for a feast," said the captain. "Especially that big plump one," he said, pointing at Raoul.

"You want to *e-e-e-e-eat* them?" stammered Marco. "They don't belong to you, Captain Tork. I intend to take them home and protect them."

"Protect them?"

"Yes. So dodo birds don't become extinct."

"We'll see about that!" Captain Tork shook his fist.

"Yes, we will!" replied Marco firmly.

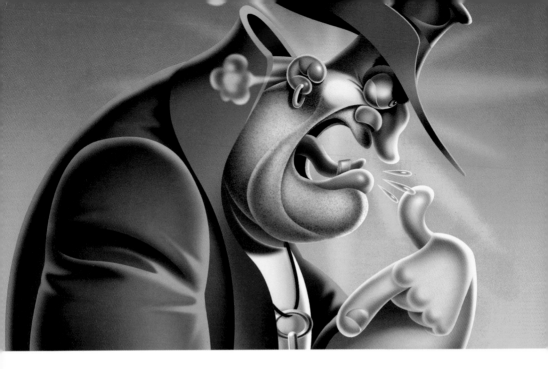

The sailors looked at young Marco in dismay. No one ever defied Captain Tork. Marco must be crazy . . . or very brave.

Captain Tork was glowing red with rage. "I'll tell you where this species is going – right into my stomach."

"You're making a serious mistake," said Marco.

"What mistake? They're just dumb birds. If they had brains, they'd fly away."

"The dodos had no enemies until we came. They didn't need to use their wings, so over the years, they've lost their ability to fly."

"Well, why don't they *run* away from us? They're too foolish to save their own necks." Captain Tork laughed.

"Who are the bigger fools, Captain? The dodos have peacefully existed here, and we've gone and wiped them off the face of the earth!"

"Enough!" Captain Tork towered over Marco. "Or I'll lock you in the ship's hold."

Marco was brave, but I could tell he was frightened. Suddenly, his eyes grew wide. I saw exactly what he saw: a key dangling from Captain Tork's neck – the key to our cage.

"But Captain. . . ." said Marco.

The captain interrupted. "No buts about it! These dodos will end up in my stomach, and that's final."

"No!" said Marco. "You must not eat them!"

"Are you giving me an order, boy?" Captain Tork grabbed Marco by the collar, and pulled him close. "One more word, and you'll spend the voyage home hanging by your feet in the hold."

I shook my head. Why had Marco provoked the captain like that? He'd only made things worse.

"Now, go help the others prepare for our departure."
With that, the captain dropped Marco onto the sand.

Marco lay on the beach, hands clenched, cowering.
That seemed to please Captain Tork. He turned to the
two sailors.

"I'm starving. Let's go tell the cook to prepare a feast –
with them." He pointed to our cage.

The three sailors rowed back to the ship. Marco slowly
unclenched a fist. In his open hand was the key to our
freedom.

# CHAPTER FOUR

# Run, Cosmo, Run!

Marco looked quickly around to make sure nobody was watching. As he opened the lock, he whispered, "Listen to me carefully. I am going to let you go. Run away from here as fast as you can."

I was surprised. Only a few minutes ago, he had been talking about gardens and cages. The idea of a life of confinement was awful, but now Marco's protection was great. He was very brave.

"If you stay with me, sooner or later, you'll all end up on Captain Tork's dinner plate," Marco said.

He was right. Marco couldn't protect us from Captain Tork. When the cage door opened, I escaped first, followed by Zoe and Raoul. I took one last look at Marco and bobbed my head to thank him.

He looked dumbfounded. "Did you just nod at me?"

I nodded again.

"Now I know I'm crazy! I talk to a bird and he answers. If you understand what I'm saying, heed my advice: You must all flee to the forest. Get as far away from here as you can. And don't ever come back!"

We ran as fast as we'd ever run in our lives. Just as we reached the edge of the forest, Zoe turned for a moment and winked at Marco.

The last thing I heard before we disappeared into the trees was Marco muttering, "Did that bird . . . just . . . ? No, I must be hallucinating."

CHAPTER FIVE

# Professor Nino's Discovery

Professor Nino was so excited, he could barely stand still. He and his assistants, Suzie and Ming, were trying to finish the robot-ship.

The robot-ship was Professor Nino's life's work. For as long as he could remember, he had been studying ways to save the earth's extinct species. Today, he was going to achieve his goal. And it was all thanks to the amazing discovery he had made that fateful day. . . .

Professor Nino had been working in front of a huge computer screen that displayed all kinds of calculations, graphics, and diagrams of space. He'd been struggling with a problem when, all of a sudden, the answer jumped out at him! His ideas fell into place. Professor Nino shouted for joy.

In their office next door, Suzie and Ming, startled, almost fell off their chairs. When the professor appeared, he had only one word to say: "Incredible!"

"What's incredible?" asked Suzie. The professor's excitement was contagious.

"I've discovered a time tunnel around Earth."

"A time tunnel?" asked Ming.

"Yes, it has six gates. Each gate, when entered at the speed of light, allows you to take a leap into the past."

"You mean that you've discovered a way to travel in time?" asked Ming.

"Exactly."

"And if we travel back through time –" Suzie began.

The professor finished her thought. "We can save species that are extinct today!"

"Hurray!" cried Suzie and Ming together.

"I think what you mean is super duper awesome!" The professor was ecstatic. The three of them returned to his computer to look at his calculations.

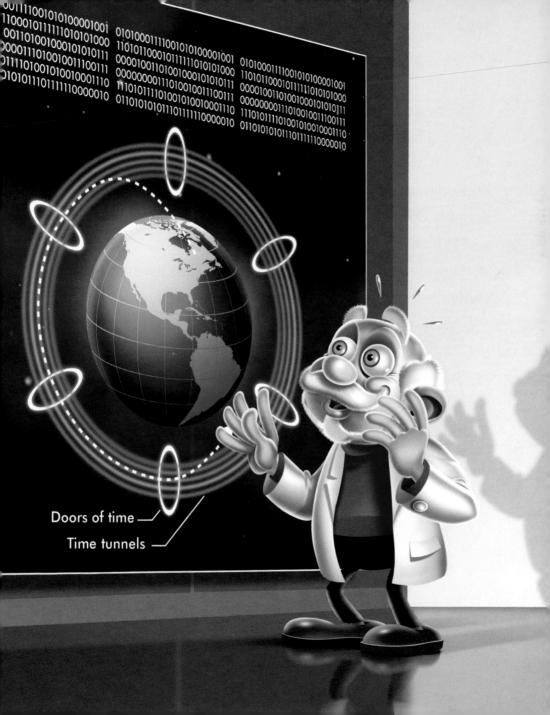

Doors of time
Time tunnels

Suzie and Ming couldn't believe what they were seeing. The professor *had* discovered a way to travel through time.

Suddenly Ming froze. "But Professor, how will we actually do the traveling through time?"

"Why, through the time tunnel, of course!"

"I understand that," said Ming. "But what kind of vehicle will actually take us through the tunnel?"

"Well, I haven't figured out what kind of spacecraft yet."

Suzie and Ming studied the computer screen.

"The spacecraft will have to be sturdy. Otherwise, the turbulence and comets and meteors will destroy it in a matter of seconds –" Suzie began.

Ming chimed in. "And it will have to travel at the speed of light!"

"And it has to use renewable energy, of course," said Suzie.

"Furthermore, if all your calculations are correct, only a small spacecraft can pass through these time gates," said Ming. "No human will be able to squeeze into such a tiny cockpit."

"Goodness me, so much to think about." The professor tugged his beard. "To sum it all up, we need an ecological spacecraft that can travel at the speed of light, survive turbulence, and that has an artificial intelligence developed enough to be able to identify and save various endangered species once it lands."

Professor Nino went to his tablet on his desk and started to draw. Suzie and Ming looked over his shoulder. A while later, he was done. Professor Nino stood up.

"Let me show you the very first sketch of 3R-V, the robot-ship."

## One year later...

After countless hours of hard work, Professor Nino, Suzie, and Ming were making the final adjustments to the robot-ship. The three scientists were nervous.

*Ah, how time flies!* thought Professor Nino. He chuckled to himself. Then he turned back to the robot-ship. Ming connected the last circuit. In a few seconds, 3R-V would come to life.

# CHAPTER SIX

# Welcome to the World, 3R-V!

As if he was waking up from a deep sleep, 3R-V slowly opened his eyes.

"Hello, 3R-V," said the professor gently.

The robot-ship looked around. "Uh, hello," 3R-V replied.

"His first words," said Suzie, and she wiped her eyes. Ming gave her a hug.

"Welcome to our world," continued Professor Nino.

"Your world?" asked 3R-V. He was still a little stunned.

Professor Nino, Ming, and Suzie watched him stand for the first time.

The professor guided him to the window and showed him the landscape outside. "We're on planet Earth."

The robot-ship studied every detail of the outdoors: the trees, the flowers, the mountains in the distance, the blue sky, and the white clouds.

After several minutes, the professor cleared his throat. "I am Professor Nino, and these are my assistants, Suzie and Ming. We designed you," he explained.

3R-V looked at each of them in turn. "What did you design me to be?"

"Your name is 3R-V, which stands for 'reduce, reuse, recycle, and vision.' You are an intelligent robot-ship that operates on renewable and non-polluting energy. You have many special features, which you will learn to use in time. For now, you should know that you're super-fast and virtually indestructible," answered the professor.

Suzie held up a mirror for 3R-V. The robot-ship seemed surprised by his reflection. He looked at his hands (each had three fingers and a thumb), his feet, and his big eyes. Then he tried opening and closing the clear bubble on his back. He activated the two turbo-jets attached to his wing-tips and rose up into the air.

"His first flight," said Suzie proudly.

3R-V quickly gained confidence. He flew over Professor Nino's desk, buzzed by Ming's head, and landed softly next to Suzie.

"You were created for a very important mission," said the professor.

3R-V perked up. "What mission?"

"We designed you to protect biodiversity."

The robot-ship looked at them, confused. "What's biodiversity?"

"Outside, there are animals and plants and insects living in balance. They're all different species, and they all need protection."

3R-V thought for a moment. "Are they in danger? Why do we have to protect them?"

"Today," began Professor Nino, "most people understand that the balance our environment provides is important to the survival of our world. We must protect all living species and work to restore their natural habitats, which human beings have destroyed over the years. We want to repair the mistakes that were made in the past."

Professor Nino continued. "Whether we realize it or not, our activities have caused the disappearance of many species. Suzie, Ming, and I are trying to find some of those extinct animals and bring them back."

"What's my part in the project?"

"You are going to travel into the past, using the time tunnel, and return with a family of each species that is now extinct."

"I'm going to voyage back in time," marveled 3R-V. "What's my first mission?"

Professor Nino pointed to his big computer screen. The image of a little monkey appeared.

"First, you'll save a red colobus family. This species of monkey is now extinct. Thanks to the time tunnel, you can travel to the year 1900, where you will collect a family of this species."

"How does the time tunnel work?"

MISS WALDRON'S
RED COLOBUS

# CHAPTER SEVEN

# Liftoff!

Next, a picture of the earth and a time tunnel appeared on the screen.

"Here's your route. First, you will propel yourself into space until you reach and enter the time tunnel. Once you're there, you must accelerate until you reach the speed of light. You must leave the tunnel at the third time gate. That will take you straight to the year 1900.

3R-V traced the route with his finger. "What if I miss the gate?"

"You'll be lost forever in the past."

"Couldn't I just make the trip back in reverse?"

"That's impossible," replied the professor. "Let me explain. While you travel back in time, we will stay in contact with you, in order to guide you home. We can only do that if we know your exact location."

"What happens if I lose contact with you?" For the first time, 3R-V was worried.

"We won't be able to calculate your return route. If this happens –"

"I'll be lost in time, and the mission will fail." 3R-V finished the sentence. He studied the diagram of Earth and the time tunnel one last time. At last, he faced the professor, Ming, and Suzie.

"I'm ready," he said bravely.

The three scientists led 3R-V outside.

Professor Nino pointed toward the sky. "That is outer space. Are you ready?"

3R-V nodded.

"Now, all I have to do is enter the trip's coordinates into your computer, " said the professor.

He opened 3R-V's control panel and punched in several numbers. Meanwhile, Suzie polished a little spot on 3R-V's right wing, and Ming tightened a screw near his nose. All three stepped back and admired their handiwork.

"Everything is in place," said Professor Nino. "Remember, leave at the *third* time gate."

3R-V activated his turbojets. Ming started the countdown: "Five, four, three, two, one. Liftoff!"

The robot-ship took off, rising up into the sky and disappearing behind the clouds. Professor Nino, Suzie, and Ming jumped for joy. Their invention worked!

Suzie wiped away a tear. "Oh, dear, how fast they grow up."

CHAPTER EIGHT

# Supper on the Run

"Uh, Captain, Sir?" said the cook. "Where are the dodos?"

Captain Tork, busy giving orders to the sailors, didn't even look in the cook's direction.

"They're in the cage, you fool!"

"*Ummm*, there aren't any dodos in that cage. The door is open and the cage is empty."

"What are you talking about? The cage can't be open. I'm the only one with the key." Captain Tork felt his neck. Then he groped in his coat pockets. "My key!" he yelled. "And where are my dodos?"

Marco stood straight and tall, his arms crossed. "They escaped. And I helped them."

"You stole my key and let my supper go? You'll pay dearly for this!" Captain Tork shoved Marco into the arms of the two sailors. "Take him to the brig!"

"I am prepared to rot in the brig, rather than see you eat the last dodos in the world," said Marco.

"Silence, you miserable little bookworm!"

"Long live free dodos!" Marco pumped a fist in the air, as the sailors dragged him away.

In a fury, Captain Tork called for a dodo hunt. He ordered his best sailors to find the dodos and bring them back.

Zoe, Raoul, and I ran through the forest. We heard the crack of leaves and branches behind us. They were coming for us.

"They're going to catch us again," gasped Raoul. He was lagging behind.

"Run, Raoul! Don't stop," called Zoe.

Just then, I realized the forest around us was familiar. We were near where our village had once stood. "Follow me!"

"Cosmo, do you have a plan?" asked Zoe.

"The river. Head for the river!"

Zoe knew what I was thinking, but Raoul, who was having trouble catching his breath, didn't understand. "Why the river?" he panted.

"Save your breath, Brother. Follow Cosmo."

We reached the river just before two hunters emerged from the woods. I leaped from rock to rock. I could hear Zoe and Raoul following behind me. Each rock was familiar, and in no time, we were across.

The hunters weren't quite so surefooted. They were the same two that had captured us before. The big hunter jumped onto the first rock and almost lost his footing. "Watch out! This is slippery," he called to the smaller sailor.

Too late. First one, then the other, plunged into the water.

We were already on the opposite riverbank.

Zoe laughed as she saw the men floundering about in the water. I pulled on her wing. "Hurry, quick! We can't stop. We have to get away before they make it to dry land."

"We have to stop soon. I really need to rest," complained Raoul.

I knew we'd have to find a hiding place. The hunters were swimming in our direction. We dove back into the forest, skipping over branches, roots, and rocks. I kept an eye out for a hiding place, and I saw the perfect spot.

"Look, there's a hollow log straight ahead!" I scrambled into the fallen tree. Raoul was behind me, but something was wrong. I heard Zoe outside.

"Move, Raoul. They're coming," Zoe's voice was urgent. "I can hear them."

But Raoul was stuck. Zoe pushed with all her might, while I tugged at him from inside. He didn't budge. "What are we going to do?" he cried.

"Don't worry. Just suck in your stomach," I said to him.

But as I tugged, something pulled Raoul out of the opening. I fell back and hit my head. I must have blacked out for a moment. When I came to, Zoe and Raoul were gone.

I groped around the inside of the hollow log, but there was no sign of my friends. Then I heard the hunters.

"Another great hunt!"

"The captain will be pleased."

I crawled out as fast as I could, ready to attack, but the hunters were already heading for the forest. They had Raoul and Zoe. Just before they all vanished, Zoe called out, "Save yourself, Cosmo! You are the very last dodo!"

# CHAPTER NINE

# Good-bye, Friends!

Despite Zoe's warning, I set out after them. My eyes were so full of tears that I kept stumbling. There had to be a way to free them. I had already lost my family and my whole village. I couldn't bear to lose my friends too.

I followed until I fell and could not go another step. Though my heart was breaking, I realized that going after them was useless. I rested until I caught my breath, and as Zoe had wanted, I turned and fled to save myself.

Suddenly, my way was blocked by a gigantic rat.
I staggered back.

I turned tail and ran back the way I had come as fast as I could. I didn't get far before two more rats emerged from the forest and grabbed me by the wings. I was trapped.

The gigantic rat, which seemed to be the leader, snarled. "What do we have here? Looks to me like a dodo."

"Hey, Chief, we just saw his two pals. Those humans were pretty happy with their catch."

The big rat approached me, menacingly. "If they're hunting you, it must be because you're a tasty treat." I tried to make myself as small as possible. "What do you say we find out, my friends?"

The other rats nodded eagerly.

"I prefer my dodos in an omelette, but since eggs are quite rare nowadays, we'll have to settle for *you* just the way you are."

The rats came closer, baring their teeth and licking their lips. Zoe's last words echoed in my head: "Save yourself, Cosmo! You are the very last dodo."

I had to survive. I pretended to faint, and the two rats released their hold on me. I quickly slipped between them, as their jaws snapped shut on empty air.

"Hurry, our dinner is getting away," shouted the chief rat. The trio was right behind me.

After a few minutes, I came to a gorge. How could I climb down it and up again in time? Then I remembered Raoul's idea from long ago. I climbed a tree, grabbed a vine, and swung across the gap.

The rats were hot on my heels. The chief rat, excited about catching me, didn't notice the gorge, until it was too late. He plunged over the edge.

He managed to grab a handhold. "Help me, you idiots!"

"But, Chief, the dodo is getting away!"

"Forget about dinner!"

On the other side of the ravine, I raced through the forest. I knew just where to go so that I would be safe from rats and hunters. The island of Mauritius is divided into two parts. One half is always sunny, and the sailors dock over on that side. The other half of the island is humid, and it rains there several months out of the year. Humans don't often go there.

I had no other choice. All I could do was repeat "Run, Cosmo, run!" to myself.

*Somewhere in time and space…*

CHAPTER TEN

# Meteor!

3R-V hurtled through space. Before he knew it, he was at the time tunnel.

"Well?" said Professor Nino into the microphone.

"Everything is going well." The time tunnel was right in front of him. As 3R-V stretched out a hand to touch it, he was sucked inside. Immediately he reached a phenomenal speed. "Wow! Now this is really flying!"

"Don't forget to count the gates!" warned the professor.

"I just saw the first one."

3R-V passed the first time gate, then the second. As he approached the third gate, he prepared himself for entry.

But, to his horror, an enormous meteor appeared, heading straight for him. He swerved to miss it.

"I almost collided with a meteor!" said 3R-V. He was spinning out of control.

"You what?" yelled Professor Nino. "I can't hear you!"

3R-V saw the third gate whiz right past him. "Oh, no! I've missed the gate!"

"Where are you?" The professor's voice was fading. "Are you there, 3R-V? Are you –"

3R-V had lost contact with Professor Nino. The robot-ship had passed the point of no return. Dizzy from the turbulence, 3R-V was spinning toward an unknown time period, somewhere deep in the past.

At the fifth gate, he flew out of the time tunnel and hurtled toward Earth. 3R-V was lost forever in the past.

CHAPTER ELEVEN

# Scram!

I had to stop and rest. Though I had heard neither humans nor rats following me, I had run all night. I was safe for the moment, with nothing but silence surrounding me.

"It's the calm before the storm," I whispered, knowing that it was exactly what Zoe would have said. Thinking of her and Raoul made me weep again. The fact that I was the very last dodo was horrible to accept.

I was all alone in the middle of the forest, on a part of the island I didn't know. I had grown up where the sun shone every day. Here, everything was gray and bleak. Exhausted, I huddled at the foot of a tree. My last thoughts before I fell asleep were of a sunlit days when I played happily with my friends.

I was awakened by the crack of twigs underfoot. Before I could sit up, the three rats popped out of the bushes and circled me. I was caught again.

"There you are!" said the giant rat. "So this is where you've been hiding!"

The memory of my friends gave me courage. "Scram!" I yelled as loud as I could. "Leave me alone or I'll kick your tails!" I looked all three of them evenly in the eyes.

"Oh look, the little bird is angry. Isn't he cute?" The chief rat's lips drew back in a frightening smile.

Furious, and with nothing to lose, I jumped onto the fat rat and pecked him as hard as I could with my beak. The other rats threw themselves at me. I fought back with all my might, but I was growing weaker.

Just then, the chief rat let out a low growl. His friends must have heard it too. As if on cue, they slowly backed off and ran away. What could have frightened them away?

# CHAPTER TWELVE

# For All the Dodos Who Disappeared

I gave myself a moment to relish the relief. I turned to see who had saved me, but all I saw was a shadow in the mist. I knew it must be a human. Marco! Marco had come to my rescue.

I was about to jump for joy, but the figure that stepped out of the gloom had a dodo feather stuck in his hat, a shiny earring, and meaty shoulders. Captain Tork!

I was still tired from fighting the rats, but I started to run nonetheless. I didn't get far. Captain Tork leaped in front of me, shaking a net.

"So, you little morsel, you thought you could escape me," he thundered.

Captain Tork advanced, a menacing look in his eyes. But, the thought of my friends, my parents, my neighbors, and all the other dodos, who were now gone, gave me a burst of energy. I would not let the captain catch me.

Maybe I could dart between his legs. But Captain Tork had thought of that. He held his net with one hand, and with the other, he grabbed my foot and hoisted me into the air. I twisted my body and bit his thumb with all the strength in my beak.

"OWWW!" The captain jerked his hand away and dropped me. But I was no better off than before. He was still there, and I was still cornered. I was too tired to fight any longer. I said a silent apology to the dodos that had already been wiped out and prepared to give up.

"When I think of how those rats almost got *my* dinner! Never mind, you'll make a fine breakfast." The captain laughed, showing off his yellow teeth.

I resigned myself to my fate and closed my eyes.

*THWOK!* Suddenly, I was knocked to the ground by a great weight. I opened my eyes cautiously. Captain Tork was lying right on top of me. I crawled out from under him.

Captain Tork was out cold with a big lump on his
head. I couldn't see the thing that had knocked him over,
and I didn't care. I was relieved. I sensed something
moving near me. Through the mist, I saw another strange
shape. This time it wasn't human, but it must have been
what had saved me.

I approached the shape and found a glittering, silver
creature teetering on his feet. It looked as though Captain
Tork's head had broken the creature's fall.

# CHAPTER THIRTEEN

# The Meeting

"Are you all right? Did you break anything?" I asked the strange creature.

"Ouch! That was quite a landing, but I'm still in one piece," answered 3R-V shakily. "Professor Nino was right. I *am* tough."

Something about the stranger's voice was reassuring. I wrapped my wings around him. "Thank you! You saved my life."

I stepped back to take stock of the odd creature. His smooth, shiny surface looked like the material that humans used to make their tools and weapons. But he didn't seem like any of the humans I had come across before – he didn't frighten me.

"Who are you? Where did you come from?"

"I'm 3R-V, the robot-ship."

"Robot-ship?"

"Yes. I was invented for space flight and time travel."

I had so many questions that I didn't know where to begin. But they'd have to wait because the robot-ship wobbled and fell over.

"Oh dear," he said. "I guess I'm still a bit groggy."

I helped him up, and in no time, he was much better. "What are you doing here?"

"It's a bit complicated." 3R-V scratched his dome. "Where did I land? What year is this?"

"You must really be groggy! Everyone knows that we're on the island of Mauritius, and it's the year 1750."

"What am I going to do? I missed the third time gate, and now I'm lost. This isn't where – or when – I'm supposed to be! My mission will never succeed."

I backed away, surprised by the robot-ship's reaction. But he pulled himself together quickly and began to talk to the sky.

"Professor? Ming? Suzie? Are you there?"

I was worried that his landing had damaged his brain. "Why are you talking to yourself?"

"I'm trying to contact my inventors. I'm from the future. I was traveling through a time tunnel in space, when a meteor came out of nowhere. When I swerved to get out of its way, I missed the time gate that I was supposed to go through. That's when I lost contact with the professor and his assistants."

Every word he said sounded like gibberish. "You're not lost in the past. I told you what year we're in and what island you're on."

3R-V thought about that, and it seemed to make him feel better. Then it was his turn to ask questions.

"Who are you, and what are you doing all alone in this dark, dreary place?"

My heart began to ache all over again. "I am Cosmo the Dodo. I've lost my only friends, and now I'm the last of my species."

"There are no other living dodos?"

"None. They've all been killed." I had such a feeling of dread that I slid to the ground. 3R-V sat down next to me. He was just as discouraged as I was.

"We're both in a tough spot." 3R-V patted his dome thoughtfully. Abruptly, he got to his feet.

"Why don't I search my records? Maybe I can dig up some information on dodos. Then I'll be able to help you, even if I don't make it back to the time period I was supposed to find." Without another word, 3R-V folded himself up and closed his eyes. He looked like a big round shell.

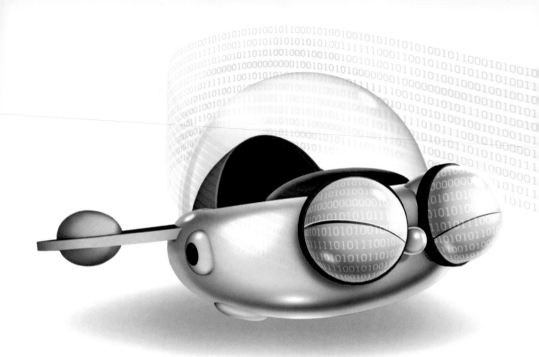

I called his name, but there was no response. The robot-ship was closed up tighter than a clam. But under his eyelids, I could see rapid movement. At least I knew he was alive, so I waited patiently. Several minutes passed without his moving. I was growing worried, so I shook him gently.

"3R-V?" He still didn't respond. I was about to shake him again, when he stirred. Lights flashed and 3R-V opened his eyes and jumped to his feet.

"What is it? Did you find anything?" I asked.

"I have it! My job is to protect biodiversity. I may have failed in my mission to save the monkeys, but I'm sure the professor would want me to help you! After all, I was built to save all endangered species."

I was more confused now than ever. 3R-V continued. "I don't know how to get back to Professor Nino in the future, but I do know how to help you right now. I'm sorry, Cosmo, but dodos have disappeared. There aren't any left on Mauritius or anywhere else on planet Earth."

I nodded, though I didn't know what a planet was.

"But, there are other planets in the universe. Some even look like Earth. They have forests and a warm climate. If there are other dodos out there, our best chance of finding them is to visit those planets."

"Okay. But what's a planet? What's the universe?"

"Climb aboard! Soon, you'll find out all about planets and the universe."

3R-V's glass dome opened with a gentle *whoosh*. I hesitated.

"What's wrong?"

"I don't want to leave. Everything I ever loved was on this island."

"I know your past was sad, but you can't change it. You *can* change your future. But not if you stay – it's too dangerous. From now on, we'll have a great adventure!"

"None of my kind has ever left the island. I'll be the first."

"But you're the last of your kind. Your only hope is to find somewhere else to live."

The robot-ship was right. I had nothing left to lose. It was time to take control of my own fate.

"I'll miss this beautiful place."

3R-V smiled and held out his hand. I took it and climbed aboard. Panel lights flashed brightly. Although everything was unfamiliar, I felt safe inside 3R-V's glass bubble. I had found a new friend and was no longer alone.

# CHAPTER FOURTEEN

# Another Flight!

Suddenly, a net enveloped us. Captain Tork was awake!

"Aha! Hold it right there, you metal weirdo! You aren't going to steal my supper!"

I was panic-stricken, but 3R-V was calm. He stood his ground, staring at the captain.

Captain Tork fastened the net around us with one swift movement. 3R-V jumped to his feet, winked at Tork, and blasted off into the air without any warning. The captain held fast to his net, his feet dangling above the ground.

3R-V zipped through the trees. For the first time in my life, I was flying. I twisted around and looked at Captain Tork. He grimaced as branches and leaves whipped by his head, but he didn't let go.

"Hold tight! We're going into warp speed!" 3R-V warned me.

At the edge of the forest, the robot-ship veered and zoomed toward the beach. Once he had a clear path, the spaceship dipped and swooped. One barrel roll followed another as we spun and looped across the sky. Still, Captain Tork held on with an iron fist.

"He's stubborn, isn't he?" said 3R-V. "But he doesn't stand a chance."

3R-V flew at full tilt toward the clouds. I heard a loud snap. The super-speed had finally snapped the netting! The captain cried out as he fell into the sea.

I took one last look at my home. As we flew higher and higher, my island got smaller and smaller until it was

"Yes, a planet is a large round body that continually revolves around a star, such as the sun. "

"Are there many planets?"

"Look ahead of you. That should answer your question."

"It's so beautiful – and immense. So this is what's beyond Earth's sky."

"And this is only a small part of the universe. Each one of the stars you see is like a sun," explained 3R-V.

I was amazed at everything I saw.

"These suns shine on thousands of planets. Some of them must have conditions like Mauritius. And some may have dodos there as well. We'll travel from planet to planet, searching for other dodos. It will be a new beginning for both of us."

"That will be our mission!" I vowed.

Together, 3R-V and I took off at the speed of light.

THE ADVENTURES OF
COSMO
THE DODO BIRD

THE CLIMATE MASTERS

THE ADVENTURES OF
COSMO
THE DODO BIRD

THE CHAIN REACTION

*For more cosmic fun, go to*
*www.cosmothedodobird.com*

### THE QUEST OF THE LAST DODO BIRD
The last dodo bird on Earth, Cosmo, is running for his life when something amazing happens. 3R-V, a robot-spaceship from the future, hurtles down from space and rescues him. 3R-V's mission is to travel back in time and save endangered species from extinction. 3R-V and Cosmo, set off to explore the universe in search of other dodos.

### THE TRAVELING PLANET
Cosmo the dodo bird and his friend 3R-V find and land on a traveling planet that has been blown out of its galaxy by a huge galactic tornado. Before they know it, they, along with a strange group of castaways, are in excitement. The new friends learn from each other and realize they have been given a second chance to protect their new environment.

### THE CLIMATE MASTERS
When a strange object is discovered on the traveling planet, the friends find that they can change the climate with the push of a button! It doesn't take long before they have a planet-sized problem on their hands. The balance of nature has been destroyed, and Cosmo comes up with the solution to stop the damage before it's too late . . . or does he?!

### THE CHAIN REACTION
The adventure continues when it becomes apparent that the climate is now completely out of control. One catastrophe leads to another, putting the friends' lives in danger. With the traveling planet in ruins, should they abandon their once-beautiful home or put selfishness aside and work to restore it?